D1284422

.996 by Nord-Süd Verlag AG, Gossau Zürich, Switzerland
.ed in Switzerland under the title *Pauli! Du schlimmer Pauli!*
anslation copyright © 1996 by North-South Books Inc.

.ts reserved. No part of this book may be reproduced or utilized in
form or by any means, electronic or mechanical, including photocopying,
cording, or any information storage and retrieval system,
without permission in writing from the publisher.

First published in the United States, Great Britain, Canada,
Australia, and New Zealand in 1996 by North-South Books,
an imprint of Nord-Süd Verlag AG, Gossau Zürich, Switzerland.
First published in paperback in 1999.
Distributed in the United States by North-South Books Inc., New York.

Library of Congress Cataloging-in-Publication Data
Weninger, Brigitte.
[Pauli! Du schlimmer Pauli! English]
What have you done, Davy? / Brigitte Weninger ;
illustrated by Eve Tharlet ; translated by Rosemary Lanning.
Summary: Davy, an energetic bunny, makes his sister and brothers mad at him
when he accidentally wrecks their things, but with his mother's encouragement,
he manages to make things right.
[1. Behavior—Fiction. 2. Family life—Fiction. 3. Rabbits—Fiction.]
I. Tharlet, Eve, ill. II. Lanning, Rosemary. III. Title.
PZ7.W46916Wh 1996
[E]—dc20 95-52221

A CIP catalogue record for this book is available from The British Library.

ISBN 1-55858-581-8 (trade binding) 10 9 8 7 6 5 4 3 2
ISBN 1-55858-582-6 (library binding) 10 9 8 7 6 5 4 3 2 1
ISBN 0-7358-1082-6 (paperback) 10 9 8 7 6 5 4 3 2 1
Printed in Belgium

For more information about our books, and the authors and artists
who create them, visit our web site: http://www.northsouth.com

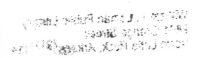

What Have You Done, Davy?

Brigitte Weninger
Illustrated by Eve Tharlet

Translated by
Rosemary Lanning

A MICHAEL NEUGEBAUER BOOK

NORTH-SOUTH BOOKS / NEW YORK / LONDON

William F. Laman Public Library
2801 Orange Street
North Little Rock, Arkansas 72114

Davy was woken by the sun shining into his burrow. It was going to be a lovely day.

He jumped out of bed, his head full of plans. He would eat his breakfast as fast as he could, and run down to the riverbank to make bark boats with his friend Eddie.

But Davy started watching spiders spinning silken threads and took far longer to eat his breakfast than he had intended. He was the last little rabbit to leave the burrow.

Davy raced across the meadow, whacking the grass with a stick, sending up sparkling fountains of dew. Then, suddenly, the stick flew out of his hand, sailed through the air, and landed right in front of his sister, Daisy.

"What have you done, Davy?" she shrieked. "You've broken
  my toys!"
"S-sorry," stammered Davy, and he ran away as fast as he could.

Davy came hurtling around the old oak tree at the edge of the forest—and ran straight into a wall!

Thumpety, bumpety, bump! Branches tumbled down all around him.

"What have you done, Davy?" shouted his brother Donny. "That's my playhouse you've smashed. It took me ages to build, and now you've ruined it!"

He picked up a branch and brandished it like a club, but Davy didn't wait to get hit. He ran away and hid, deep in the forest.

It was some time before Davy plucked up the courage to come out of hiding and look around. He liked the forest. The ground here was covered with soft, springy cushions of moss. Davy bounced from one to another.

Bounce, bounce . . . oh, no! Down he went into a deep, deep hole. "What have you done, Davy?" shouted his brother Dan. "You've wrecked my secret burrow! Just wait till I get my hands on you!" But Davy kicked himself free and ran away before his big brother could catch him.

Davy came back to the burrow at
lunchtime. His stomach was rumbling,
but there was no one at home.
Davy crept into the larder—just to see
what was in there, not to eat anything,
of course! This is what he saw: a turnip,
some carrots, a bag of oats, and a big
bowl of blueberries. Round, shiny, sweet-
smelling blueberries. Yum yum! Davy's
mouth watered. He tasted one berry,
then another. . . . They were so delicious
that he couldn't stop.
Suddenly Davy heard voices. He hid
behind the larder door.

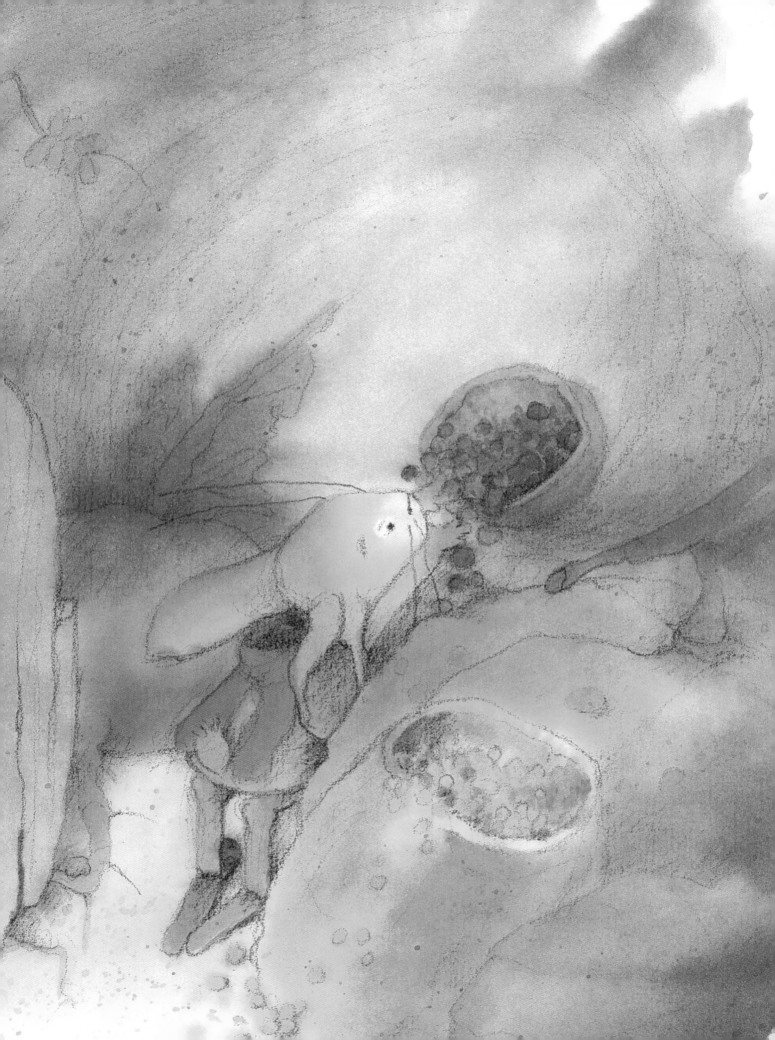

Mother Rabbit had come back, and Daisy was with her.
"Davy has been so naughty today," Daisy said. "He broke my toy
animals. I'd like to break his toys, too!"
Davy's heart thumped. That wasn't fair! He hadn't done it on
purpose!

Before Mother could reply, Donny came in, shouting, "Davy has been so naughty today! He knocked down my playhouse. You should never let him go outside again!"
Davy was stunned. It had only been an accident.

Then Dan came rushing in and said, "Davy has been so naughty today. He made my secret burrow collapse! When I find him, I'm going to pull his ears!" Davy shivered. He hadn't even known the burrow was there until he fell into it!

"Davy is a very bad bunny," said Daisy crossly.

"Davy doesn't mean to be bad," said Mother. "He is a dear, clever bunny, but sometimes he's careless. I'll have a serious talk with him when he comes home. Where is the little rascal?" Nobody knew.

"Well," said Mother. "He'll be here soon enough. Come and
eat, children. I've brought you some fresh dandelion leaves,
and there are blueberries for a special treat."
Oh, no! thought Davy. The blueberries!
Davy trembled with fright. He had meant
to try only a few of them.

Mother went into the larder and saw the empty bowl.
Then she saw Davy, cowering behind the door, with a
purple stain around his mouth.
"There you are, you little scamp!" she said.
Suddenly Davy remembered what he usually did to
make Mother smile. He opened his arms wide, put his
head on one side, and said, "How about a kiss?"
"Certainly not," replied Mother severely. "No kisses
today. We are all much too angry with you. What do
you have to say for yourself?"

There was silence. Then Davy gulped and said, very quietly,
"I'm sorry. I'm really, really sorry. I didn't mean to do any of
those bad things."
"Saying sorry isn't good enough!" said his sister and brothers.
"We'll only forgive you when you make up for all the
damage you have done."

"What do you mean?" asked Davy.

"You must mend all my broken animals," said Daisy.

"And fix my playhouse," said Donny.

"And help me dig out my burrow," said Dan.

Davy turned to his mother.

"But I wanted to play with Eddie today!" he protested.

"Well, that will have to wait until tomorrow," said Mother calmly. "Because after you mend Daisy's animals, fix Donny's playhouse, and dig out Dan's burrow, you're coming with me to pick blueberries!"

So Davy had a very busy afternoon.

He mended Daisy's toy animals, and even found a
pretty feather to make one of them into a bird.

He hammered stakes into the ground next to the old oak tree
and helped Donny to weave twigs between them. The playhouse
they made was even better than the old one.

He dragged basket after basket of heavy soil away
from the deep burrow that Dan had dug.

And then he hopped into the forest with Mother to pick
fresh blueberries for supper.

That night Davy was very, very tired. He was dozing in a
corner when Father Rabbit came home.

"Well," said his father, "what have you done today, Davy?
You look tired out."

Davy hugged his father and told him: "I made new fir-cone
animals for Daisy and built a playhouse with Donny. Then
I helped dig out Dan's burrow, and I've just been picking
blueberries with Mother."

"You did all that in one day?" said Father. "My, you have
been busy!" And he said to Mother, "It sounds as if Davy
has been especially good and clever today."

William F. Laman Public Library
2801 Orange Street
North Little Rock, Arkansas 72114

Mother, Daisy, Donny, and Dan all laughed.
They laughed so hard that Davy had to laugh too.

He stood up, opened his arms wide, and said,
"How about a kiss, now?"

And they kissed him, one by one.